the ELF on the SHELF

Dream big dreams
Always believe!
Aebersold

A Christmas Tradition

by Carol V. Aebersold and Chanda A. Bell
illustrated by Coë Steinwart

www.ccaandb.com

Have you ever wondered how Santa could know
if you're naughty or nice each year as you grow?
For hundreds of years it's been a big secret.
It now can be shared if you promise to keep it.

At holiday time
Santa sends me to you.
I watch and report
on all that you do.
My job's an assignment
from Santa himself.
I am his helper,
a friendly scout elf.

The first time I come to the place you call home
you quickly must give me a name of my own.

Once you are finished my mission can start.
What will you call me-Markle or Zart?
Will it be Foddle, Criddle, or Clyde?
Fisbee's cute, too, but you must decide.

Each night while you're sleeping
to Santa I'll fly
to the North Pole
right through the dark sky.
Of course Christmas magic
helps me to be quick.
I laugh with my friends
and report to Saint Nick.

I tell him if you have been good or been bad.
The news of the day makes him happy or sad.
A push or a shove I'll report to "the Boss,"
but small acts of kindness will not be a loss.

In the car, at the park,
or even at school
the word will get out
if you broke a rule.

I'll be back at your home before you awake,
and then you must find the new spot I will take.
You'll jump out of bed and come running to see:
who'll be the first to spy little old me?

Maybe the kitchen, the bathroom, or den
is where you will find me, your special elf friend.
I can hide on a plant, a shelf, or a frame.
Where will I be? Let's make it a game.

There's only one rule that you have to follow
so I will come back and be here tomorrow:

Please do not touch me. My magic might go,
and Santa won't hear all I've seen or I know.

I won't get to tell him that you've said your prayers,
or helped to bake cookies,
or cleaned off the stairs.
How will he know how good you have been?
He might start to think you forgot about him.

I can't speak to you, so says Santa Claus.
All of us elves have to follow his laws.

I'll listen to you. Tell me your wishes.
Would you like a game or some tiny toy dishes?
The gleam in my eye and my bright little smile
shows you I'm listening and noting your file.

The final decision with Santa now rests.
What do you think?
Will you get your request?

The night before Christmas my job's at an end.
The rest of the year with Santa I'll spend.

So blow me a kiss and bid me farewell.
I'll fly away when I hear Santa's bell.
Of course I will miss you,
but wait 'til next year.
When the holidays come I'll again reappear.

Until then I wish every girl and each boy
a Christmas of peace and a year full of joy.

This tradition began for the

_____

family

on _____ , 20____ .

We welcomed our elf

by choosing the name:

_____ .

ISBN-13: 978-0-9769907-9-6

Printed and bound in China.
9 8 7 6 5 4 3 2 1

www.elfontheshelf.com

1174 Hayes Industrial Drive
Marietta, GA 30062
www.ccaandb.com